THE STORY OF THE
GOLDEN STATE WARRIORS

THE NBA:
A HISTORY
OF HOOPS

THE STORY OF THE
GOLDEN STATE
WARRIORS

NATE FRISCH

CREATIVE EDUCATION

Published by Creative Education
P.O. Box 227, Mankato, Minnesota 56002
Creative Education is an imprint of The Creative Company
www.thecreativecompany.us

Design and production by Blue Design
Art direction by Rita Marshall
Printed in the United States of America

Photographs by Corbis (Bettmann), Getty Images
(Andrew D. Bernstein/NBAE, Garrett W. Ellwood/NBAE,
Jesse D. Garrabrant/NBAE, Walter Iooss Jr./Sports
Illustrated, George Long/Sports Illustrated, Melissa
Majchrzak/NBAE, NBAPhotos/NBAE, Hy Peskin/Sports
Illustrated, Christian Petersen, Dick Raphael/NBAE,
Kent Smith/NBAE, Visions of Our Land, Rocky Widner/
NBAE), Newscom (Christopher Chung/ZUMA Press, John
McDonough/Icon SMI, Susan Tripp Pollard/Contra Costa
Times/MCT)

Library of Congress Cataloging-in-Publication Data
Frisch, Nate.
The story of the Golden State Warriors / Nate Frisch.
p. cm. — (The NBA: a history of hoops)
Includes index.
Summary: An informative narration of the Golden State
Warriors professional basketball team's history from its
1946 founding in Philadelphia, Pennsylvania, to today,
spotlighting memorable players and events.
ISBN 978-1-60818-430-9
1. Golden State Warriors (Basketball team)—History—
Juvenile literature. I. Title.

GV885.52.G64F75 2014
796.323'640979461—dc23   2013037449

CCSS: RI.5.1, 2, 3, 8; RH.6-8.4, 5, 7

First Edition
9 8 7 6 5 4 3 2 1

Cover and page 2: Guard Stephen Curry
Pages 4&5: Forward Corey Maggette
Page 6: Guard Monta Ellis

TABLE OF CONTENTS

COURTSIDE STORIES

INTRODUCING...

GOLDEN BEGINNINGS

CALIFORNIA'S BAY BRIDGE CONNECTS THE CITIES OF SAN FRANCISCO AND OAKLAND.

Before 1848, California was sparsely populated and valued primarily for basic resources such as furs and lumber. Then, near a sawmill owned by John Sutter, gold was discovered, and prospectors from all walks of life swarmed on California, hoping to strike it rich. Many came by sea, and the small coastal settlements of San Francisco and Oakland soon boomed and became synonymous with dreams of a better life. Today, the vast Bay Area is still known for its diversity and progressive thinking, and it includes some of the most affluent areas in the United States.

About a century after the California Gold Rush began and on the opposite side of the country, a professional basketball team called the Philadelphia Warriors was among the founders of the new Basketball Association of America (BAA). Although other professional leagues

ED "MR. BASKETBALL" GOTTLIEB (FAR RIGHT) PUT TOGETHER A WINNING PHILADELPHIA TEAM.

already existed, the BAA was the first to focus on major cities and huge arenas. The idea was grand, but it meant that clubs had high overhead costs. The Warriors struggled to turn a profit in Philadelphia, Pennsylvania, and in 1962, they hoped to change their fortunes by heading west to California's alluring Bay Area. Fittingly, the team eventually became known as the Golden State Warriors.

In 1946, Edward Gottlieb—a stout man more accustomed to organizing and promoting sporting events than to running a team— became the Philadelphia Warriors' first manager and head coach. Gottlieb quickly demonstrated an eye for talent, signing revolutionary forward Joe Fulks from Kentucky's Murray State University. In the BAA's inaugural season, Fulks led the league in scoring with 23.2 points per game. "He made one-handed shots, jump shots, right-handed [and] left-handed set shots from a distance, driving shots, hooks with his right or left hand," said Gottlieb. "He was also basketball's first jump shooter."

"Jumpin' Joe" was paired with fellow rookie forward Howie Dallmar, one of the league's top assist men. The duo led the Warriors to the first

COURTSIDE STORIES

A PERFECT START

It's always best to make a good first impression, and that's just what the Warriors did when they won the Basketball Association of America's very first league championship. The BAA started up in 1946 with 11 teams, including the newly created Philadelphia Warriors. The players on the Warriors' roster had little to no experience playing professional basketball, but in such a new league, they didn't need a lot. "Jumpin' Joe" Fulks, a 25-year-old rookie forward out of Murray State University, led the league in scoring with 23.2 points per game; his total of 1,389 points was nearly one-third of the total points scored by the Warriors all season. After finishing second in the Eastern Division with a 35–25 record, Philadelphia defeated the St. Louis Bombers in the first round of the playoffs. They then trounced the New York Knicks in the second round to advance to the first-ever BAA Finals, where they rolled over the Chicago Stags, four games to one. In winning the inaugural BAA title, the team that became today's Golden State Warriors got off to the perfect start.

11

WILT CHAMBERLAIN

POSITION CENTER
HEIGHT 7-FOOT-1
WARRIORS SEASONS
1959–65

He was big, dominant, and possibly the best player ever to play the game of basketball. The NBA record books are littered with his name. He scored the most points ever in a single game with a whopping 100-point effort versus the New York Knicks in 1962. He pulled down 55 rebounds in one 1960 game, which is also tops all-time. Furthermore, he's the only center ever to have led the league in assists (during the 1967–68 season). Wilt "The Stilt" Chamberlain stood 7-foot-1, and despite his lean build, he was both powerful and athletic. Opposing teams frequently tried to double- or even triple-team Chamberlain to stop him, but his size and strength allowed him to play through those tactics and still dominate. When he retired in 1973, he was the all-time NBA scoring leader, and he still holds the league mark for most career rebounds with 23,924. Chamberlain's greatest adversary was Celtics center Bill Russell, who tipped his cap to Chamberlain, saying, "Wilt was the greatest offensive player I have ever seen." The record books agree.

TOM W RANGERS \ DETROIT
WED RANGERS \ CHICAGO
THURS MANHATTAN \ ST PETER S
N Y U \ FORDHAM
FRI BOXING TERRELL \ ZECH

KNICKS

13

BAA championship in 1947, overwhelming the Chicago Stags four games to one. Philadelphia reached the finals again in 1948, but the Baltimore Bullets—a new addition to the league—came out on top. The Warriors' third campaign was a disappointment, as they were bounced from the playoffs after two straight losses in the opening round. After the season, the BAA and the competing National Basketball League (NBL) merged to form the NBA in 1949, with the Warriors and 16 other clubs as inaugural members.

ife in the NBA was a struggle for the Warriors at first. After another losing season, the Warriors bounced back in 1950–51 to capture the top spot in the Eastern Division with a 40–26 record, but they were knocked out in the first round of the playoffs. In 1952–53, the Warriors plummeted to 12–57. Luckily, two new arrivals, guard Paul Arizin and high-scoring center Neil Johnston, were on the scene to help new coach George Senesky take the team back to the top. Philadelphia catapulted to a 45–27 record in 1955–56, and then captured its first NBA championship, beating the Fort Wayne Pistons four games to one in front of record crowds.

After winning the 1956 championship, Philadelphia discovered that talent had improved around the league, and the Warriors were no longer top dogs. Despite solid play from Arizin and forward Joe Graboski, the team came up short in the playoffs the next two seasons and fell to 32–40 in 1958–59. As the competition in the NBA got stiffer, the Warriors found themselves in need of a player who could separate them from the pack once again.

NATE THURMOND

POSITION CENTER / FORWARD
HEIGHT 6-FOOT-11
WARRIORS SEASONS
1963–74

Nate Thurmond was a big guy who could do it all. Thurmond followed the great Wilt Chamberlain as a star center for the Warriors, and while he wasn't as flashy as his predecessor, he was arguably more versatile than Chamberlain. Opponents had to beware of Thurmond down low, because he was a fierce defender who excelled at both blocking shots and snatching rebounds. As he gained experience, he also became an offensive force, which made him one of the game's greatest all-around players. On October 18, 1974, as a member of the Chicago Bulls, he became the first NBA player ever to record a "quadruple-double" (notching double-digit totals in 4 statistical categories), with 22 points, 14 rebounds, 13 assists, and 12 blocks in a single game. Especially on defense, Thurmond had few peers. "His statistics aren't overwhelming, but his presence on the court is unbelievable," said Warriors guard Walt Hazzard. "As for blocking shots, I've seen guys get offensive rebounds and then go back 15 feet to make sure they can get a shot off. They know Nate is there."

LOCAL TREASURE

WILT CHAMBERLAIN AND BILL RUSSELL'S MAN-TO-MAN RIVALRY TURNED LEGENDARY.

n 1955, the NBA added a rule allowing teams to exchange their first-round pick in the league's annual draft for the right to claim any local college player in hopes of keeping homegrown talent close to their fans. The Warriors took advantage of this rule in 1959 and snatched up 7-foot-1 and 275-pound Philadelphia native Wilt Chamberlain as their "territorial" selection in that year's NBA Draft. "He could do whatever he wanted to do on a basketball court," Warriors coach Frank McGuire said of the talented center. "No player, not even Bill Russell, could stop him."

Bill Russell, the great defensive center for the Boston Celtics, couldn't exactly stop Chamberlain, but his Celtics teams repeatedly came out on top, as they would win 9 of the 10 NBA championships in the 1960s. During those years, Chamberlain and Russell frequently clashed with physical battles on both ends of the floor in what was

RICK BARRY

POSITION FORWARD
HEIGHT 6-FOOT 7
WARRIORS SEASONS
1965-67, 1972-78

One wouldn't expect an NBA player who uses a granny shot on free throws to be an intimidating force on the court, but that's just what Rick Barry was throughout his career. Barry was a fierce competitor who wanted to win at all costs. His intensity sometimes got on the nerves of his opponents and even his own teammates as he pushed everyone around him to the limit, but there was no question he played to win. With a sharp outside shot and a knack for cutting through the lane to either score a layup or earn two foul shots, Barry was one of the most prolific scorers in NBA history. In 1974–75, he averaged 30.6 points per game to lead the Warriors to an NBA championship. He led the league in free-throw percentage six times in his career and finished his NBA career as a 90 percent free-throw shooter—now sixth-best in NBA/ABA history. "He's an intense competitor, whether it's basketball, golf, checkers, or anything else," said Warriors coach Bill Sharman. "He just doesn't want to lose."

quite possibly the NBA's best rivalry ever at the center position.

Six years of not making it to the NBA Finals, and another heartbreaking loss to the Celtics in the 1962 Eastern Division finals, proved to be too much for Philadelphia fans. Attendance waned, Gottlieb sold the Warriors to a group of San Francisco investors, and the Warriors headed west to play at their new home, San Francisco's Cow Palace. Chamberlain continued to dominate on the West Coast, leading the NBA in scoring for the fourth straight year, but the 1962–63 San Francisco Warriors finished a mere 31–49.

n 1963, Alex Hannum was hired as San Francisco's head coach. Hannum knew his team had talent. Guards Guy Rodgers and the intense Al Attles formed a solid backcourt, and young and aggressive center/forward Nate Thurmond played a big role as a rebounder and shot blocker. But the coach depended mainly on his star center. "For us to win," Hannum explained, "Wilt has to play like Bill Russell when we're on defense and play like Wilt Chamberlain when we're on offense."

The Warriors powered their way to the 1964 NBA Finals behind the dominance of Chamberlain and the hot shooting of forward Tom Meschery, who averaged 16.8 points per game during the team's playoff run. However, the Warriors fell to the mighty Celtics once again, four games to one. After San Francisco got off to a poor start the next season, the Warriors traded Chamberlain back to Philadelphia, where a new NBA team—the 76ers—had developed from the relocation of the former Syracuse Nationals. For all his record-setting years with the Warriors, Chamberlain never had managed to bring the franchise a

championship trophy.

The Chamberlain trade allowed two new stars to rise in San Francisco. The first was Thurmond, who quickly evolved into one of the NBA's best centers. The other was forward Rick Barry, who joined the Warriors as a frail-looking youngster in 1965. Over the next few seasons, Barry would prove capable of scoring almost at will from anywhere on the court, and his deadeye shooting would earn him the nickname "The Golden Gunner."

Led by Barry and Thurmond, the 1966–67 Warriors again reached the NBA Finals, where they faced off against the 76ers and their old teammate, Chamberlain. Barry poured in an average of 40.8 points per game in the Finals, but the Warriors couldn't stand up to Philadelphia's powerful inside attack, and the 76ers prevailed in 6 games.

The next season, Barry left to join a team in the new American Basketball Association (ABA), and Thurmond assumed the spotlight mostly by himself. Powered by a low-post offense that revolved around Thurmond and forward Rudy LaRusso, who had a career season with 21.8 points per game, the Warriors made it to the Western Division finals before losing to the Los Angeles Lakers in a 4-game sweep.

RICK BARRY

COURTSIDE STORIES

DODGING THE BULLETS

Everyone loves an underdog, so when the Warriors made it all the way to the 1975 NBA Finals to face the Washington Bullets, they had to be feeling the love. For most of the season, NBA fans had focused on the battle in the Eastern Conference between the Bullets and the Celtics. The two powerhouses had each posted a superb 60-22 record, while the Warriors had finished with a respectable, but certainly not intimidating, 48-34 mark. When playoff time arrived, the Warriors were playing their best ball and fought through the first two rounds of the playoffs to square off against the heavily favored Bullets, who featured such stars as guard Kevin Porter and forward Elvin Hayes. Every game was intense, but the Warriors stunned the Bullets with smothering team defense and clutch scoring by Rick Barry to pick up three straight victories. In Game 4, the Warriors fell behind but were able to scratch their way back to win 96-95. The Finals' Most Valuable Player (MVP) award went to Barry, who claimed afterwards, "It has to be the greatest upset in the history of the NBA Finals."

ATTLES'S ERA

HOT-HANDED JEFF MULLINS RECORDED MORE THAN 12,000 POINTS WITH THE WARRIORS.

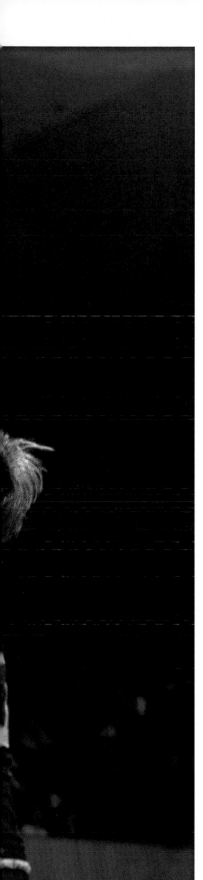

After San Francisco made early exits from the playoffs in 1968 and 1969, Al Attles took over as a player/coach with 30 games remaining in the 1969–70 season. Shortly after getting a new coach, the franchise got a revised image. Since arriving in the Bay Area, the team had played home games in three different cities—San Francisco, Oakland, and San Jose. Finally, in 1971, the team settled into the Oakland Coliseum Arena and dropped its exclusive San Francisco affiliation in favor of a name that it hoped would broaden its fan base, becoming the Golden State Warriors.

The renamed and resettled Warriors were a team with some talent. Thurmond anchored the inside along with forward Clyde Lee, while guard Jeff Mullins paced the Warriors in scoring. In 1972, the Warriors' Golden Gunner returned as Rick Barry came back from the ABA for a

THE GRANNY SHOT

It's how most little kids first shoot a basketball and how an old lady would probably let the ball fly. The famous "granny shot" in basketball involves holding the ball with both hands below one's waist, bending at the knees, and throwing the ball upward in an underhand motion. It's simple, but it looks rather silly. It's not a shot one would expect to see in an NBA game, but two Warriors stars found it a worthwhile technique at the free-throw line. Wilt Chamberlain, a center who struggled mightily to make free throws, tried the granny shot, but he didn't stick with it for long. Rick Barry, a slick-shooting forward of the 1960s and '70s, on the other hand, used it almost exclusively when he stepped to the "charity stripe." The Hall-of-Famer was a 90 percent career free-throw shooter using the granny style. "I didn't [originally] want any part of it, but my father drove me nuts until I tried it," Barry said. "And amazingly, it worked. Nobody ever teased me, but it's hard to tease somebody when the ball keeps going in."

second stint in Warriors gold and blue. Still, the Warriors of the early '70s were successful in the regular season but sputtered in the playoffs.

The 1974–75 season changed all that. Before the season, Thurmond was traded to the Chicago Bulls for center Clifford Ray, a defensive specialist. The Warriors then added guards Charles Johnson and Butch Beard and smooth rookie forward Jamaal Wilkes to the starting lineup. With Coach Attles preaching a fast-break offense and a gambling defense, the Warriors fought their way to a 48–34 record.

Although their record was not phenomenal, the Warriors headed into the 1975 playoffs with confidence, and in the first two rounds, they toppled the Seattle SuperSonics and the Bulls to reach the NBA Finals. Golden State faced the heavily favored Washington Bullets in the championship round, but in a stunning upset, the Warriors swept the series in four straight games to win the title. "We cared about winning and did whatever we could to win," said Barry. "It was an atmosphere you'd like to see more professional teams have. I defy anyone to find anything like it."

The next season, Barry, Wilkes, and swingman

FORWARD PURVIS SHORT WAS KNOWN AS "RAINBOW MAN" FOR HIS HIGH-FLOATING JUMP SHOT.

RUN T.M.C.

In the mid-1980s, a three-man hip-hop group called Run D.M.C. shook up the music industry with hits such as "Walk This Way" and "You Be Illin'." Several years later, in the early '90s, the Warriors had their own super-trio shaking things up on the basketball court. With a high-octane offense, the Warriors were led by three very different stars who quickly became known around the league as "Run T.M.C." Tim Hardaway, Mitch Richmond, and Chris Mullin were the fuel that powered coach Don Nelson's "run-and-gun" offense. Hardaway was the lightning-quick ball handler, Richmond excelled at slashing to the basket, and Mullin played the role of outside sharpshooter. In 1990–91, all 3 players averaged more than 20 points per game in leading the team to a 44–38 record and a first-round playoff series win over San Antonio. Their combined 72.5 points-per-game average that season made them the highest-scoring trio in NBA history. Despite failing to make it to the NBA Finals, Run T.M.C. brought a new level of excitement to the Oakland Arena for Warriors fans.

MITCH RICHMOND

> ## "WE CARED ABOUT WINNING AND DID WHATEVER WE COULD TO WIN. IT WAS AN ATMOSPHERE YOU'D LIKE TO SEE MORE PROFESSIONAL TEAMS HAVE. I DEFY ANYONE TO FIND ANYTHING LIKE IT."
>
> — RICK BARRY ON THE WARRIORS

Phil Smith powered the Warriors to a 59–23 record—an all-time franchise best. But the team couldn't get past the Phoenix Suns in the Western Conference finals. After losing in the second round the next year to the Lakers, the Warriors entered into the bleakest stretch in franchise history, missing the playoffs every year from the 1977–78 through 1985–86 seasons.

Still, the Warriors teams of the early 1980s were not without stars. Young center Robert Parish was beginning to flourish before the Warriors dealt him to the Celtics in 1980 for two draft picks. Golden State used 1 of those picks to select center Joe Barry Carroll, who put up 6 seasons of at least 17 points per game for the Warriors. The trade would haunt Warriors fans, though, as they watched Parish become a three-time champion with the Celtics. Explosive forward Bernard King and charismatic guard World B. Free stepped into the spotlight during the 1981–82 season and helped the Warriors to a 45–37 record, but the team missed the playoffs by a single game.

The next season, King left for greener pastures in New York, and an injured Warriors lineup stumbled to a 30–52 finish. Despite consistent scoring from shooting guard Terry Teagle, Golden State finished with losing records in each of the next three seasons before new ownership and a new coach arrived in 1986. It was then that radio mogul Franklin Mieuli, who had owned the team since its relocation to California, sold it to an ownership group led by business entrepreneurs Jim Fitzgerald and Dan Finnane. The new owners wasted little time in making changes, naming George Karl the new head coach before the next season.

The move paid off, as the Warriors made the playoffs for the first time in nearly a decade with a 42–40 mark. After sneaking past the Utah Jazz in a hard-fought, five-game series, Golden State came up short against the Lakers, losing four games to one. The 1987–88 season was a big step backward, as the team could muster only a 20–62 record. Coach Karl resigned late in the season, leaving Ed Gregory with the coach's clipboard until Don Nelson took over.

AL ATTLES

POSITION GUARD, COACH
HEIGHT 6 FEET; WARRIORS
SEASONS AS PLAYER 1960–
71, AS COACH
1969–83

As a player, Al Attles was nicknamed "The Destroyer." He was never the fastest or most athletic player on his team, but he was a tenacious defender and a rugged enforcer who was feared throughout the league for his temper and physical play. When he became the Warriors' head coach, he showed off his strength as a strategist. He liked his teams to be fast and in remarkable shape so that they could wear out their opponents. Hired in 1969, Attles was one of the first African American coaches in the NBA, and his battle with the Bullets and their coach, K. C. Jones, in the 1975 Finals was pro basketball's first championship matchup between two black head coaches. Attles did not play favorites as coach and would frequently use his lesser-known players as much as his stars if he felt it would help win a game, and his teams tirelessly attacked their opponents on each end of the court. "That's really where the team took on Al's personality," said Warriors forward Jamaal Wilkes. "We were quick, we were tough, and we challenged people."

TALENT AND TANTRUMS

ALL-STAR LATRELL SPREWELL HAD AN EXPLOSIVE PRESENCE BOTH ON AND OFF THE COURT.

The Warriors needed to develop a team identity, and Nelson was just the coach to give them one. In 1988–89, Nelson designed a wide-open offensive attack that revolved around two sharpshooters, forward Chris Mullin and young guard Mitch Richmond. In 1989, the Warriors drafted fast, slick-dribbling point guard Tim Hardaway and continued to improve as they developed an exciting, high-scoring style of play that kept fans riveted. In 1990–91, Golden State won a playoff series against the San Antonio Spurs before losing in the second round to the Lakers. The next year, the Warriors traded Richmond away and lost in the first round.

In the 1992 NBA Draft, the Warriors acquired forward Latrell Sprewell. "Spree," as he was known to Golden State fans, never seemed to tire on the court as he flew from end to end. In his second season, Sprewell teamed up with a

ANDRIS BIEDRINS

BARON DAVIS

MATT BARNES

RUNNING DOWN THE MAVERICKS

It's always handy to have an ace up your sleeve. When the eighth-seeded Warriors matched up against the top-seeded Mavericks in the first round of the 2007 playoffs, no one figured they had a ghost of a chance. What most people forgot was the Warriors' ace. Don Nelson had been the Mavericks' coach just two years prior, and he knew Dallas's strengths and weaknesses. The Warriors started a small lineup that was fast and aggressive. The bigger Mavericks couldn't keep up with them when Golden State had the ball and couldn't get away from their pesky defense on the other end of the court. Point guard Baron Davis led the way for the Warriors, averaging 25.3 points per game in the series. The Warriors out-hustled and outsmarted the Mavericks to win the series four games to two, completing what many consider to be the NBA's biggest postseason upset since the Warriors beat the Bullets in 1975. "We made NBA history tonight," said Davis, "and that's the best thing about it. We did it as a team."

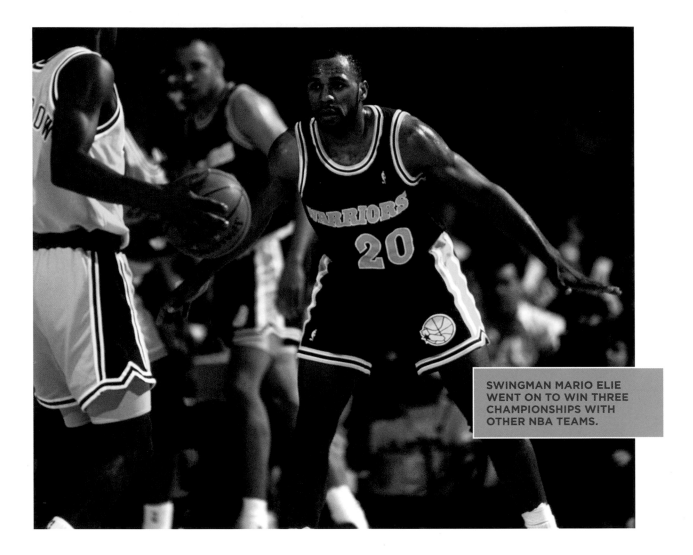

new scoring threat, brawny rookie forward Chris Webber, to lead the Warriors to a 50–32 record and a playoff berth. The Warriors were unable to get past Phoenix in the first round, though, as star forward Charles Barkley and the Suns swept Golden State in three straight games.

Unfortunately, just when it seemed Golden State was approaching true contender status, things fell apart. Coaches and players feuded,

and in 1994, Webber was traded to the Bullets, and Nelson stepped down. By the end of the 1994–95 season, the Warriors were 26–56, and after Hardaway was traded away, only Sprewell remained as a star.

After two more losing seasons, the Warriors brought in new head coach P. J. Carlesimo in 1997. Soon after, during a practice, Carlesimo and the temperamental Sprewell got into an

CHRIS MULLIN

POSITION FORWARD / GUARD
HEIGHT 6-FOOT-6
WARRIORS SEASONS
1985–97, 2000–01

Everyone loves a comeback, and Chris Mullin's early career was an inspiring story for the Warriors faithful and basketball fans throughout the country. Picked seventh overall by the Warriors in the 1985 NBA Draft, Mullin was a scorer with unlimited potential, but he also struggled with alcohol abuse. He proved to be a serviceable player in his first two years with the Warriors, but it wasn't until new coach Don Nelson urged him to seek treatment in 1987 that the Chris Mullin the Warriors had hoped for showed up. After his rehab, Mullin became a fitness fanatic and a tireless worker on and off the court. With a sweet left-handed jumper and outstanding fundamentals, he became a dynamic scorer and a perennial All-Star. Lacking top-level quickness, moves, or jumping ability, Mullin was one of the unlikeliest stars in the NBA. In 1992, his marksmanship touch earned him a spot on the U.S. Olympic basketball team known as the "Dream Team." Teammate Tim Hardaway was among the many left in awe by Mullin's shooting accuracy. "You pass Mully the ball," Hardaway said, "and it's an assist."

argument, and the All-Star guard physically attacked the coach. Sprewell never played for the Warriors again, drawing a one-year suspension from the NBA before being traded. Although he admitted threatening his coach's life, Sprewell was as brash in leaving town as he had been in arriving. "I made a mistake, and I'm sorry for that, but that doesn't make me a bad man," he said.

he Sprewell incident cast a lingering cloud over the Warriors, and the team missed the playoffs each of the next eight seasons. Warriors management seemed to lack a clear rebuilding plan as players and coaches were shuffled like cards in and out of the franchise. One of the few bright spots in Golden State's lineup for several years was all-purpose forward Antawn Jamison, who joined the club through an NBA Draft trade in 1998.

Beginning in 2001, new faces began arriving to provide hope for the Warriors faithful. Explosive guard Jason Richardson and rugged forward Troy Murphy both joined the Warriors via the 2001 NBA Draft, and the team selected

lanky forward Mike Dunleavy the following year. These three players formed a foundation in Golden State that would last for five years as they avoided the trades that had so often whisked the Warriors' best players away. The team still fell short of the playoffs the next three years, but the Warriors improved from a dismal 2000–01 season, in which they won only 17 games, to average 32.8 wins in each of the next 5 seasons.

JASON RICHARDSON'S
ATHLETICISM AND TEAM
LOYALTY MADE HIM A
CROWD FAVORITE.

DIALING UP THE SPEED

THE WARRIORS CAPITALIZED ON BARON DAVIS IN THEIR QUEST FOR THE PLAYOFFS.

The 2004–05 season appeared to be more of the same when the Warriors lost their first six games and later suffered a nine-game losing streak. Hoping to right the ship, the Warriors made a midseason trade for point guard Baron Davis. "The thing I love about Baron is he delivers the ball on time," said new Golden State head coach Mike Montgomery. "You don't have to wait, you don't have to reach. The ball is delivered on time, and it's delivered to you. He's a true point guard."

In addition to playing team ball and pesky defense, Davis was a dangerous scorer, capable of attacking the rim or hitting outside jumpers. He also refused to give up. Despite Golden State's being well out of playoff contention, Davis led the Warriors to a remarkable 14–4 record over the final 18 games. The wins kept coming early in 2005–06. Unfortunately, an injury to Davis doomed the Warriors, who

DON NELSON IMPLEMENTED HIS "NELLIE BALL" STRATEGY WITH ANDRIS BIEDRINS'S HELP.

fizzled to a 34–48 mark. Following the collapse, Don Nelson was brought back as coach.

For the 2006–07 campaign, Nelson revived the old run-and-gun style of offense to capitalize upon the talents of Davis, Richardson, and second-year guard Monta "Mississippi Bullet" Ellis. The Warriors also swung a midseason trade that sent Murphy and Dunleavy to the Indiana Pacers in exchange for more athletic forwards: the multitalented Al Harrington and long-range bomber Stephen Jackson. Lean, young Latvian center Andris Biedrins took the place of Golden State's older, lumbering big men. With an up-tempo offense in place, the Warriors became the league's second-highest-scoring team, bringing excitement back to the renamed Oracle Arena and sneaking into the playoffs with a 42–40 season record.

This was the Warriors' first postseason appearance in 13 years, and few expected them to withstand the Western Conference's top seed, the 67–15 Dallas Mavericks, in the first round. The Warriors shocked everyone by ousting the Mavericks four games to two. In the series' final game, Golden State clobbered

TIM HARDAWAY

POSITION GUARD
HEIGHT 6 FEET
WARRIORS SEASONS
1989–96

Tim Hardaway's game was a classic case of "now you see him, now you don't." At only six feet tall, Hardaway was short by NBA standards, but he had energy and confidence to spare. His signature move was a crossover dribble in which he would fake a drive in one direction, stop, and then head the other way so quickly that defenders would frequently fall over themselves trying to follow him. The only safe defense against Hardaway's crossover dribble was to back off far enough, but when that happened, he'd simply sink the outside shot. And when his team needed him the most, the little man with the big swagger was at his best. "When the game is on the line," said teammate Chris Mullin, "you have to wrestle him for the ball." Hardaway frequently took charge late in games for the Warriors with a variety of jumpers, aggressive drives, and fast-break buckets. "He's made more big plays, taken over more games, and led more runs than anybody we have," said Warriors coach Don Nelson. "When the hour is the bleakest, he saves the day. I think he's Mighty Mouse."

GUARD JAMAL CRAWFORD USED QUICK BALL-HANDLING SKILLS TO BLOW PAST OPPONENTS.

STEPHEN CURRY

COURTSIDE STORIES

LIKE FATHERS, LIKE SONS

Warriors star Rick Barry's NBA legacy didn't end when he hung up his sneakers or even when he turned off his broadcasting mic. Three of his sons—Jon, Brent, and Drew—all had NBA careers of their own. Although only Brent enjoyed similar success as his Hall-of-Fame father, all demonstrated a nice shooting touch and a good head for the game. Jon Barry—who had a one-year stint with the Warriors—even followed his dad's footsteps to the broadcast booth. Another Warriors sharpshooter, Stephen Curry, was the son of marksman Dell Curry. The senior Curry sank 1,245 three-pointers during a 16-year NBA career. But the younger Curry may have been the more accurate shooter, ranking second all-time in NBA three-point percentage after his first four seasons in the league. Golden State added another second-generation player when it drafted Klay Thompson, son of forward Mychal Thompson. The elder—and larger—Thompson was the first overall pick in the 1978 NBA Draft and enjoyed 12 years and 2 championships in the NBA. After just three seasons in the NBA, Klay's career looked promising as well. His 211 three-pointers in 2012–13 ranked third in the league.

Dallas by 25 points and held the league's Most Valuable Player (MVP), forward Dirk Nowitzki, to a miserable 2-of-13 shooting performance. "I don't know when I have to pinch myself or wake up from this dream," Richardson said. "This is everything I wanted. I wanted this for our fans, for our organization, for ourselves. We work hard, and we deserve it." Richardson's dream soon ended, however, as the Warriors fell to the Jazz in round two, and he was dealt away the following off-season.

The Warriors resumed their breakneck offense in 2007–08. Davis, Ellis, and Jackson each averaged more than 20 points per game as Golden State improved to 48–34. Unfortunately, the Western Conference was so competitive that the Warriors did not qualify for the playoffs. Davis then left town, and the leaderless Warriors won just 29 games in 2008–09.

oping to rebuild, Golden State traded away the aging Jackson and drafted Stephen Curry out of Davidson College. Curry had a teenager's face but was a dead shot and thrived under pressure. Like Ellis, he was 6-foot-3 with a slender build, and the dynamic pair shared responsibilities as point/shooting guards and put on an entertaining show. Unfortunately, Golden State's defense struggled, and its win total fell to 26.

The Warriors hoped hard-working power forward David Lee would improve team rebounding and balance out the guard-dominated offense. Golden State continued to renovate its roster toward a half-court offensive team, drafting lanky swingman Klay Thompson and, in 2011–2012, sending Ellis to the Milwaukee

Bucks for seven-footer Andrew Bogut. Injuries prevented the center from suiting up that season, but new head coach Mark Jackson believed he had the makings of a balanced team.

In 2012–13, Curry and Thompson enjoyed the best season of their young careers, and rookie forward Harrison Barnes added athleticism and versatility. The Warriors finished with a solid 47–35 mark and a spot in the playoffs. In Game 1 against the Denver Nuggets, Lee's postseason was ended by an injury, and Golden State lost the contest on a last-second layup. But Golden State fought back, upsetting the Nuggets in six games. And although they would lose to the veteran Spurs in round two, the future looked bright for the young Warriors. "It's inspiring to think of what we were able to accomplish this year and the foundation that has been laid," Jackson said.

By the next season, Golden State had traded Biedrins and was counting on experienced players for success. Newly signed swingman Andre Iguodala led the defensive charge, while other league veterans such as forward/center Jermaine O'Neal and guard Steve Blake contributed depth. Curry emerged as the Warriors' star, representing the team at the 2014 All-Star Game.

The Warriors hit pay dirt in their first year with the BAA. They have added two NBA titles since and were always on the verge of hitting the mother lode during the Chamberlain era. While many years have passed since the Warriors of Golden State struck NBA gold, the Bay Area is still the land of opportunity and optimism, and players and fans alike know that their next big strike could happen at any time.

THOUGH A TALENTED INSIDE
PLAYER, ANDRIS BIEDRINS
STRUGGLED WITH INJURIES.

INDEX